James Fairfax McLaughin

The American Cyclops, the Hero of New Orleans, and Spoiler of

Silver Spoons

James Fairfax McLaughin

The American Cyclops, the Hero of New Orleans, and Spoiler of Silver Spoons

ISBN/EAN: 9783741117992

Manufactured in Europe, USA, Canada, Australia, Japa

Cover: Foto ©Andreas Hilbeck / pixelio.de

Manufactured and distributed by brebook publishing software
(www.brebook.com)

James Fairfax McLaughin

The American Cyclops, the Hero of New Orleans, and Spoiler of Silver Spoons

THE

AMERICAN CYCLOPS,

THE

HERO OF NEW ORLEANS,

AND

SPOILER OF SILVER SPOONS.

Dubbed LL. D.

BY

PASQUINO.

BALTIMORE: KELLY & PIET.

1868.

"A pot house soldier, he parades by day,
And drunk by night, he sighs the foe to slay."

Introductory.

—⸙❦⸙—

THE following little illustrated effusion is offered to the public, in the hope that it may not prove altogether uninteresting, or entirely inappropriate to the times. The famous pre-historic story of Ulysses and Polyphemus has received its counterpart in the case of two well-known personages of our own age and country. Ulysses of old contrived, with a burning stake, to put out the glaring eye of Polyphemus, the man-eating Cyclops, and thereby to abridge his power for cannibal indulgence; while our modern Ulysses, perhaps, mindful of his classical prototype, is content to leave the new Polyphemus safely "bottled-up" under the hermetical seal of the saucy Rebel Beauregard. Although the second Cyclops is yet alive, and still possesses the visual organ in a squinting degree, a regard for impartial history compels us to add, that the sword which leapt from its scabbard in front of Fort Fisher, has fallen from the grasp of the "bottled" chieftain, whether from an invincible repugnance to warlike deeds, like that which pervaded the valiant soul of the renowned Falstaff, or because an axe on the public grindstone is a more congenial weapon in the itching palm of a Knight of Spoons, has not yet been determined with absolute precision.

The warrior Ulysses, like his namesake of Ithaca, however widely opinion may militate upon his other qualifications, certainly deserves the everlasting gratitude of a spoon-desolated country for the strategy displayed in tearing off the plumes of the American Polyphemus, and fixing that precious flower of knighthood among the "bottled" curiosities of natural history.

The American Cyclops.

―❦❀❦―

Progressive age ! for contemplation's eye,
Thy checker'd scenes a glorious field supply ;
Time was when Mercury waved the potent wand,
And Nature brightened in the artist's hand,—
When mind's dominion round the world was thrown,
Before usurping Mammon seized the throne.
Aspiring genius, chill thy noble rage,
For baser uses rule our iron age :
Drive the hard bargain, mart for sordid gain,
And where it will not win, hold honor vain ;

"He wakes a patriot: presto, he is clad
As Fallstaff for the battle—raving mad."

THE AMERICAN CYCLOPS.

To lofty subjects bring the narrow view,
Shift with each scene, and principle eschew.
Are these the elements of man's success?
Go where the busy throng all onward press:
Ay, there they flourish and will long remain,
Till virtue purge the haunts where vice doth reign.
Not to the few the moral taint's confined,
But in its boundless range infects mankind;
'Twere idle to upbraid the good old plea—
Might governs all, the rest were mock'ry.
The plumpest fly a sparrow's meal provides—
The heartless bird its agony derides:
"Nay," quoth relentless Sparrow, "you must die,
For you, weak thing, are not so strong as I."
A Hawk surprised him at his dainty meal,
In vain the Sparrow gasped his last appeal;

"Wherefore, Sir Hawk, must I, thy victim, die?"

"Peace," quoth the Hawk, "thou art less strong than I."

Grimly an Eagle viewed the state of matters,

Swoops on Sir Hawk, and tears his flesh to tatters:

"Release me, King, and doom me not to die;"

The Eagle said, "thou art less strong than I."

A bullet whistled at the victor's word,

And pierced the bosom of the lordly bird;

"Ah, tyrant!" shrieked he, "wherefore must I die?"

The Sportsman said, "thou art less strong than I."

And thus the world to might becomes the dower,

While justice yields before remorseless power.

When distant ages rise to view our times,

Whate'er betide our *silv'ry* flowing rhymes,

THE AMERICAN CYCLOPS.

The brave we sing—Bœotian of the East

Will still survive to spread the mimic feast.

'Tis said in fables that Silenus old

To Midas lent the fatal gift of gold;

But Terminus, the god of rogues, has giv'n

Our hero gold unbless'd of man or heav'n.

'Mid all the tyrants of our age and clime,

He stands alone in infamy and crime;

Not e'en Thersites of the cunning tribe,

Gloried in guile like him we now describe.

Born of a race where thrift, with iron rod,

Taught punic faith and mocked the laws of God;

Where stern oppression held her impious reign,

And mild dissent was death with torturous pain;

His youth drank in the lessons of his race,

Which stamp'd their impress on his hideous face.

Beattie ad Cruel Bethel.

Old England's bard with epic fire illum'd

Tartarean pits, where fiends with darkness gloom'd ;

But 'mid th' infernal host this face had shone,

Grimmest of all 'neath dread Armageddon.

The outward form proclaimed the inner man,

And frightened virtue fled where it began ;

The heart, the head, there devils might fear to dwell,

Lest in their depths there lurked a deeper hell.

Does fiction, fancy, gild the picture drawn,

Hate cloud our judgment, truth give place to scorn ?

Go seek the answer in the youth at school—

He scoffs at church and laughs at human rule.

A beggar,* he plays his *role* with brazen cheek,

With equal ease *insurgent* or a "sneak."

---

* He entered College in his sixteenth year as a future candidate for the ministry. As he was without resources, he was compelled to do manual work to meet the expenses incurred at the Institution. The fact is creditable.

"Leaves gallant Winthrop to his mournful fate.
But takes the field when haply 'tis too late."

A theologian, without doctor's chair,

He dons the gown t' escape the task of prayer.

"Heresiarch recant, or leave the school:"

A recantation proved the knave no fool.*

Behold him later in another sphere,

Where thieves abound and murderers appear;

Tricked out in low and meretricious art,

He plays with skill the pettifogger's part;

Chicanery's brought to succor darkest crime,

Too basely foul t' expose in decent rhyme.

Oh! shades of Littleton and Murray rise,

Where Webster trod and Choate all honor'd lies—

---

* Many instances are related of his insubordination at school and disputes with superiors. One of the preachers having advanced the opinion that only one in every hundred Christians would, perhaps, be saved, our hero drew up a theological petition asking leave to vacate his seat in church, very candidly regarding himself as among the number that would be lost. A public reprimand for his smart irreverence was the only answer vouchsafed the unfledged Doctor.

Ye Vow

"Our hero vowed Magruder's works to take,
Whereof the books no mention deign to make."

THE AMERICAN CYCLOPS.

Rise to behold the satyr in their place,
Who points the moral of his clime and race;
And if decay and shame may wake thy grief,
Weep for New England cursed by such a chief.

Oh! hapless hour, when from the stormy North,
This modern Cyclops marched repellent forth,
To slake his thirst for blood and plundered wealth,
Not as the soldier, but by fraud and stealth;
To waft the gales of death with horror rife
On helpless age, and wage with women strife:
To leave at Baltimore and New Orleans
The drunkard's name, or worse, the gibbet's scenes;
To license lust with all a lecher's rage,
And stab the virtue of a Christian age:

"Born of a race where thrift, with iron rod,
Taught punic faith and mocked the laws of God;
     *   *   *   *   *   *   *   *
His youth drank in the lessons of his race,
Which stamp'd their impress on his hideous face."

This single crime will fix a beastly name,

Fresh in immortal infamy and shame.

Whence comes his martial fame, who thus has soar'd,

While thousands fell and deadly cannon roar'd ?

The *raw militia* of his native State

Had taught him war and made our hero great.

A pot-house soldier, he parades by day,

And drunk by night, he sighs the foe to slay ;

In vision sees the future road to fame,

The bale-fires burn and cities wrapped in flame :

The gathered treasure of a teeming land

Glitters and falls beneath his blood-stained hand ;

Plantations smiling, palaces all bright,

Stuff'd with their wealth of plate, dance to his sight,

And drunken Polyphemus* grimly swoons,

---

* *Monstrum et horrendum, informe, ingens, cui lumen ademptum.* Virg. Æneid. lib. iii.

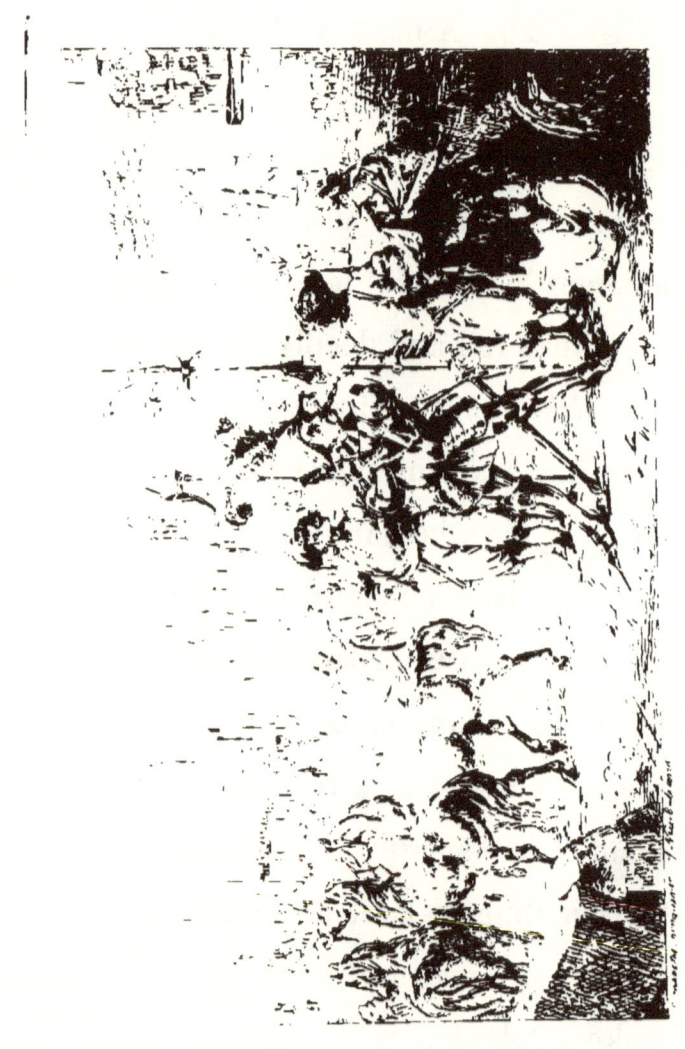

As heir expectant of unnumbered spoons.*

He wakes a patriot; presto, he is clad

As Fallstaff for the battle—raving mad.

Lo! Baltimore becomes the first emprise,

When Gilmor's scandal shock'd the men at Guy's:

"To horse, to horse," our hero drunk exclaims,

"I'll crush rebellion—give the town to flames."

The faithful groom the pawing steed attends,

The maudlin Cyclops all oblique ascends;

But ere the lambent flames consume the town,

The Cid unhorsed. like Bacchus. topples down.

Old Juno's goose erst saved imperial Rome,

But Rebel whisky saves the Rebels' home.

Next comes the dismal order—'tis from Scott—

---

* The people of a captured city were subjected to fines and levies and open plunder, and in some instances imprisoned at hard labor with ball and chain.

Dominicles encountering ye breakfast

"Fraternal discord cease."

"Leave Baltimore." He blew a warlike trump,
And marched to conquest—conquest of a pump!
Like Falstaff, seeks repose and dreams of glory,
While Bethel's thunder peal'd another story ;
Leaves gallant Winthrop to his mournful fate,
But takes the field when haply 'tis too late.
Wrath gnaws his bowels, and with words profane,
He swore an oath, as once the Queen of Spain
Vowed the same garment *malgrè* wear and tear,
Till Ostend fell she would forever wear.
Our hero vowed Magruder's works to take,
Whereof the books no mention deign to make ;
For well we know the batt'ries poured their thunder,
While wise Sir Spoons sought easier paths to plunder.
But *Io Bacche !* Victory comes at last—
Our doughty chief in New Orleans is cast ;

The donkey stole the lion's skin and brayed,
And Farragut our Cyclop's fortune made.
Where are the trophies of our Yankee brave?
The lecherous order, and poor Mumford's grave;
Ship Island's tortures, Mrs. Phillips' cell,
For mercy's reign the cruelty of hell;
A Shylock brother—a Prætorian band—
A starving city and a plundered land:
These are his triumphs—Fisher was his shame,—
Oh! triumph worse than is the coward's name.
" I'll blow Fort Fisher 'mong the region kites!"
Oh, glorious thought! but ere the fort ignites,
Our Cyclop's sailed away infirm of will,.
And saucy Fisher flash'd defiance still.
" Far better I were *hermetically* seal'd,
Than homeward borne upon a bloody shield."

"But hold, enough; no further we'll pursue
The modern Haynau. "Bottled" Chief, adieu."

"Fort Fisher be my epitaph!" 'Tis meet,

For long ago it gave thy winding sheet.

But hold, enough; no further we'll pursue

The modern Haynau. "Bottled" Chief, adieu.

Haply my country's freedom still remains,

And with the night have passed oppression's chains :

Oh, may the storms which settle o'er our land

Be gently lifted by th' all-saving Hand ;

The dove return ; fraternal discord cease,

And millions join the Jubilee of Peace !